Letters and Sounds

BASED ON **TIMOTHY GOES TO SCHOOL** AND OTHER STORIES BY

ROSEMARY WELLS

ILLUSTRATED BY MICHAEL KOELSCH

VIKING

Cover and interior illustrations copyright © Rosemary Wells, 2001 • Interior illustrations by Michael Koelsch • Text copyright © Penguin Putnam Inc., 2001
Educational consultant: John F. Savage, Ed.D. • All rights reserved • Library of Congress Catalog Card Number: 00-055254 • ISBN: 0-670-89651-9

Hilltop School

DORIS

NORA

CLAUDE

FRANK

FRANK

A B C D E F G H I J K L M

TIMOTHY'S class is singing the alphabet song while Mrs. Jenkins points to each letter. Can you sing along? As you sing each letter, point to it on the alphabet chart.

The Next Step

Can you name some letters of the alphabet when they are out of order? Give it a try:

S M Q B E

Timothy and Yoko are learning to write their names. What letters are in each of their names? Count the letters in each of their names. Which name has more letters? Which name has fewer? Write your name on a piece of paper. What letters are in your name?

 The Next Step

Now write your name and the name of a friend on a piece of paper. Do you know the letters in each name? Count the letters in each name. Which name has more letters? Which name has fewer letters?

Timothy and his friends play a game called I Spy.

h my little eye something beginning with the letter M," says Timothy.

BARS begins with the letter M," says Yoko.

s thinking of MONKEY BARS," says Timothy. "Now it's Yoko's turn."

h my little eye something beginning with the letter J," says Yoko.

GYM!" yells Claude.

at I was thinking of," says Yoko.

," says Claude. "Now it's my turn. I spy with my little eye something

g with the letter S."

guess what Claude is thinking of? What do you see in the playground

is with the letter S?

e Next Step

Spy in the room you are in right now using the letter T. Can the person you are

with guess the thing you have in mind in three tries?

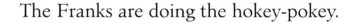

The Franks are doing the hokey-pokey.

> *You put your right hand in,*
> *you put your right hand out,*
> *you put your right hand in,*
> *and you shake it all about.*
> *You do the hokey-pokey*
> *and you turn yourself around,*
> *that's what it's all about!*

(For other verses, substitute the following for "right hand": *left hand, right foot, left foot.*)

Doris wants to play, but she's not sure she knows her right from her left. Do you?

Hold up your right hand. Hold up your left hand. Hold up your right foot. Hold up

your left foot. Now you're ready to do the hokey-pokey, too!

 The Next Step

How well do you know your right from your left? Put your left hand on your right
shoulder. Put your right hand on your left knee. Touch your left ear with your right hand.

Timothy's mother is reading to him from a book of Mother Goose rhymes.

> *Hickory, dickory, dock,*
> *The mouse ran up the clock.*

DOCK and CLOCK rhyme. Words that rhyme end with the same sounds. DOCK and CLOCK both end with OCK. "Can you think of another word that rhymes with CLOCK?" Timothy's mother asks.
"SMOCK rhymes with CLOCK," says Timothy.
"Very good!" says Timothy's mother. "You are right. SMOCK does rhyme with CLOCK."
Which of the things pictured on the opposite page rhyme with CLOCK?

The Next Step

Of the words BAT, CAT, and DOG, which two words rhyme? Why? Which word doesn't rhyme? Why?

8

"All words have beats to them," Mrs. Jenkins tells the class.
"Listen to my name: Jen-kins. Can you hear the two beats?
Tap your foot once for each of the beats in my name: Jen-kins.
Nora has two beats, also. Tap once for each of the beats in
her name: No-ra."

"My name has three beats," says Timothy. "Tim-o-thy."

"Very good," says Mrs. Jenkins. "Let's all tap once for each
beat in Timothy's name: Tim-o-thy."

You can practice beats, too. Tap your foot once for each of the
beats in the following names: Do-ris, Claude, Yo-ko.

The Next Step

How many beats are there in your name? Say your name and tap your foot once for each
beat. How many beats are in the names of people in your family? Say their names and tap
once for each beat.

Timothy and his father are shopping at the supermarket.

"Look, Timothy," says his father. "Letters are all around us. The words on the labels tell us what is in the containers."

"I see a letter I know," says Timothy. "There's an M."

"Very good," says his father. "That's a milk carton. M is the first letter in the word MILK."

"Now I see a J," says Timothy.

"Yes," says his father. "That's a juice bottle. J is the first letter in the word JUICE. Now let's look for other letters you know."

Look at the labels on the food containers with Timothy.

Can you point to any letters that you know?

 The Next Step

Next time you are in the supermarket, play the alphabet game. Look for each letter of the alphabet on a label or sign in the store.

At music time, Timothy chooses the banjo and Claude chooses the bells.

"Listen," says Timothy. "Both of our instruments begin with the same sound: BANJO and BELLS."

"You're right," says Claude. "BANJO and BELLS both start with the B sound."

Which of the things pictured in the box below start with the B sound?

 **The Next Step**

Can you think of any other words that start with the B sound?

"I know a magic trick," Fritz tells Nora. "I can turn a bat into a hat."

"You cannot," says Nora. "That's impossible."

"I can too!" says Fritz. "And I can turn a dog into a hog and a hen into a pen."

"Prove it," says Nora.

Fritz really can turn a bat into a rat. How? By changing the first letter of the word BAT from B to R. He can turn a dog into a hog by changing the first letter of the word DOG from D to H. He can turn a hen into a pen by changing the first letter of the word HEN from H to P. If Fritz wanted to change a bag into a rag, how would he do it?

 ## The Next Step

You can be a magician, too! By changing their first letters, what can you turn the following words into? CAT BUG HOT

"Stand up, everybody," Mrs. Jenkins says. "We're going to play a game."

"Yay," says Timothy. "I love games!"

"I'm going to say two words," says Mrs. Jenkins. "If they rhyme, I want you to jump. If they don't rhyme, I want you to bend over. Ready?"

"Ready!" everyone yells.

"BOAT, COAT," says Mrs. Jenkins.

Doris bends over, but everyone else jumps. "Oops," she says.

"That's okay, Doris," says Mrs. Jenkins. "You'll get it next time. Here are two more: FACE, HAND."

Everyone bends over.

"Good job," says Mrs. Jenkins.

"Here are two more words: ROSE and NOSE."

If you were in Mrs. Jenkins's class, would you jump or bend over?

 **The Next Step**

Here are more pairs of words. Jump if they rhyme and bend over if they don't rhyme:
RICE and MICE; CAKE and BALL; HOPE and ROPE.

The school day is nearly over.

"I want to tell you something before you go," says Mrs. Jenkins. "Tomorrow is A day. Everyone should bring in something that starts with the letter A for show-and-tell."

"I'm going to bring my ant farm," says Claude.

"Eew, I hate ants," says Nora. "I'm going to bring my toy alligator."

"I'm going to bring an acorn," says Timothy. "I will look for one on my way home from school."

Look for things in the picture on the opposite page that start with the letter A.

How many can you find?

 The Next Step

If you were in Timothy's class, what would you bring for A day?

23

Letter to Parents and Educators

The early years are a dynamic and exciting time in a child's life, a time in which children acquire language, explore their environment, and begin to make sense of the world around them. In the preschool and kindergarten years, parents and teachers have the joy of nurturing and promoting this continued learning and development. The books in the *Get Set for Kindergarten!* series were created to help in this wonderful adventure.

The activities in this book are designed to be developmentally appropriate and geared toward the interests, needs, and abilities of pre-kindergarten and kindergarten children. After each activity, a suggestion is made for "The Next Step," an extension of the skill being practiced. Some children may be ready to take the next step; others may need more time.

Research has shown that success in early reading is related to an awareness of the sounds that make up spoken words and a knowledge of the letters of the alphabet. *Letters and Sounds* is intended to help children become familiar with some of these sound-symbol connections in an enjoyable, hands-on manner. Language learning should also include frequent sharing of stories and poems, discussing the meaning of new words, and talking about children's experiences.

Throughout the early years, children need to be surrounded by language and learning and love. Those who nurture and educate young children give them a gift of immeasurable value that will sustain them throughout their lives.

John F. Savage, Ed.D.
Educational Consultant